SIXTY SONNETS

WILLIAM
SHAKESPEARE

SIXTY SONNETS

penguin books

PENGUIN BOOKS

Published by the Penguin Group
Penguin Books USA Inc., 375 Hudson Street,
New York, New York 10014, U.S.A.
Penguin Books Ltd, 27 Wrights Lane,
London W8 5TZ, England
Penguin Books Australia Ltd, Ringwood,
Victoria, Australia
Penguin Books Canada Ltd, 10 Alcorn Avenue,
Toronto, Ontario, Canada M4V 3B2
Penguin Books (N.Z.) Ltd, 182–190 Wairau Road,
Auckland 10, New Zealand

Penguin Books Ltd, Registered Offices:
Harmondsworth, Middlesex, England

Published in Penguin Books 1995

ISBN 0 14 60.0075 7

Printed in the United States of America

From fairest creatures we desire increase,
That thereby beauty's rose might never die,
But as the riper should by time decrease,
His tender heir might bear his memory;   *4*
But thou contracted to thine own bright eyes,
Feed'st thy light's flame with self-substantial fuel,
Making a famine where abundance lies,
Thyself thy foe, to thy sweet self too cruel.   *8*
Thou that art now the world's fresh ornament,
And only herald to the gaudy spring,
Within thine own bud buriest thy content,
And, tender churl, mak'st waste in niggarding.   *12*
   Pity the world, or else this glutton be,
   To eat the world's due, by the grave and thee.

When forty winters shall besiege thy brow,
And dig deep trenches in thy beauty's field,
Thy youth's proud livery, so gazed on now,
Will be a tottered weed of small worth held: *4*
Then being asked where all thy beauty lies,
Where all the treasure of thy lusty days,
To say within thine own deep-sunken eyes,
Were an all-eating shame and thriftless praise.   *8*
How much more praise deserved thy beauty's use,
If thou couldst answer, "This fair child of mine
Shall sum my count, and may my old excuse,"
Proving his beauty by succession thine.   *12*
   This were to be new made when thou art old,
   And see thy blood warm when thou feel'st it cold.

Then let not winter's ragged hand deface
In thee thy summer ere thou be distilled.
Make sweet some vial; treasure thou some place
With beauty's treasure ere it be self-killed.   *4*
That use is not forbidden usury
Which happies those that pay the willing loan;
That's for thyself to breed another thee,
Or ten times happier be it ten for one.   *8*
Ten times thyself were happier than thou art,
If ten of thine ten times refigured thee:
Then what could death do if thou shouldst depart,
Leaving thee living in posterity?   *12*
   Be not self-willed, for thou art much too fair,
    To be death's conquest and make worms thine heir.

O, that you were yourself, but, love, you are
No longer yours than you yourself here live;
Against this coming end you should prepare,
And your sweet semblance to some other give.   *4*
So should that beauty which you hold in lease
Find no determination, then you were
Yourself again after your self's decease,
When your sweet issue your sweet form should bear.   *8*
Who lets so fair a house fall to decay,
Which husbandry in honor might uphold
Against the stormy gusts of winter's day
And barren rage of death's eternal cold?   *12*
   O, none but unthrifts! Dear my love, you know,
   You had a father; let your son say so.

Shall I compare thee to a summer's day?
Thou art more lovely and more temperate.
Rough winds do shake the darling buds of May,
And summer's lease hath all too short a date.   *4*
Sometime too hot the eye of heaven shines,
And often is his gold complexion dimmed;
And every fair from fair sometime declines,
By chance, or nature's changing course, untrimmed;   *8*
But thy eternal summer shall not fade,
Nor lose possession of that fair thou ow'st,
Nor shall Death brag thou wand'rest in his shade,
When in eternal lines to time thou grow'st.   *12*
    So long as men can breath or eyes can see,
    So long lives this, and this gives life to thee.

A woman's face, with Nature's own hand painted,
Hast thou, the master mistress of my passion;
A woman's gentle heart, but not acquainted
With shifting change, as is false women's fashion;   *4*
An eye more bright than theirs, less false in rolling,
Gilding the object whereupon it gazeth;
A man in hue all hues in his controlling,
Which steals men's eyes and women's souls amazeth.   *8*
And for a woman wert thou first created,
Till Nature as she wrought thee fell a-doting,
And by addition me of thee defeated,
By adding one thing to my purpose nothing.   *12*
    But since she pricked thee out for women's pleasure,
    Mine be thy love, and thy love's use their treasure.

My glass shall not persuade me I am old,
So long as youth and thou are of one date,
But when in thee Time's furrows I behold,
Then look I death my days should expiate.   4
For all that beauty that doth cover thee
Is but the seemly raiment of my heart,
Which in thy breast doth live, as thine in me.
How can I then be elder than thou art?   8
O, therefore, love, be of thyself so wary
As I, not for myself, but for thee will,
Bearing thy heart, which I will keep so chary
As tender nurse her babe from faring ill.   12
   Presume not on thy heart when mine is slain;
   Thou gav'st me thine, not to give back again.

Let those who are in favor with their stars
Of public honor and proud titles boast,
Whilst I whom fortune of such triumph bars,
Unlooked for joy in that I honor most.   *4*
Great princes' favorites their fair leaves spread
But as the marigold at the sun's eye,
And in themselves their pride lies burièd,
For at a frown they in their glory die.   *8*
The painful warrior famousèd for might,
After a thousand victories once foiled,
Is from the book of honor rasèd quite,
And all the rest forgot for which he toiled.   *12*
   Then happy I that love and am beloved
   Where I may not remove, nor be removed.

When, in disgrace with Fortune and men's eyes,
I all alone beweep my outcast state,
And trouble deaf heaven with my bootless cries,
And look upon myself and curse my fate,   *4*
Wishing me like to one more rich in hope,
Featured like him, like him with friends possessed,
Desiring this man's art, and that man's scope,
With what I most enjoy contented least;   *8*
Yet in these thoughts myself almost despising,
Haply I think on thee, and then my state,
Like to the lark at break of day arising
From sullen earth, sings hymns at heaven's gate;   *12*
    For thy sweet love rememb'red such wealth brings,
    That then I scorn to change my state with kings.

Why didst thou promise such a beauteous day,
And make me travel forth without my cloak,
To let base clouds o'ertake me in my way,
Hiding thy brav'ry in their rotten smoke?   4
'Tis not enough that through the cloud thou break,
To dry the rain on my storm-beaten face,
For no man well of such a salve can speak,
That heals the wound, and curse not the disgrace.   8
Nor can thy shame give physic to my grief;
Though thou repent, yet I have still the loss.
Th' offender's sorrow lends but weak relief
To him that bears the strong offense's cross.   12
   Ah, but those tears are pearl which thy love sheeds,
   And they are rich and ransom all ill deeds.

No more be grieved at that which thou hast done:
Roses have thorns, and silver fountains mud,
Clouds and eclipses stain both moon and sun,
And loathsome canker lives in sweetest bud.   *4*
All men make faults, and even I in this,
Authorizing thy trespass with compare,
Myself corrupting, salving thy amiss,
Excusing thy sins more than thy sins are;   *8*
For to thy sensual fault I bring in sense—
Thy adverse party is thy advocate—
And 'gainst myself a lawful plea commence.
Such civil war is in my love and hate   *12*
   That I an accessory needs must be
   To that sweet thief which sourly robs from me.

40

Take all my loves, my love, yea take them all;
What hast thou then more than thou hadst before?
No love, my love, that thou mayst true love call;
All mine was thine, before thou hadst this more.   4
Then if for my love thou my love receivest,
I cannot blame thee for my love thou usest;
But yet be blamed, if thou this self deceivest
By willful taste of what thyself refusest.   8
I do forgive they robb'ry, gentle thief,
Although thou steal thee all my poverty;
And yet love knows it is a greater grief
To bear love's wrong than hate's known injury.   12
    Lascivious grace, in whom all ill well shows,
    Kill me with spites; yet we must not be foes.

That thou hast her, it is not all my grief,
And yet it may be said I loved her dearly;
That she hath thee is of my wailing chief,
A loss in love that touches me more nearly.   *4*
Loving offenders, thus I will excuse ye:
Thou dost love her, because thou know'st I love her,
And for my sake even so doth she abuse me,
Suff'ring my friend for my sake to approve her.   *8*
If I lose thee, my loss is my love's gain,
And losing her, my friend hath found that loss:
Both find each other, and I lose both twain,
And both for my sake lay on me this cross.   *12*
    But here's the joy: my friend and I are one;
    Sweet flattery! Then she loves but me alone.

What is your substance, whereof are you made,
That millions of strange shadows on you tend?
Since everyone hath, every one, one shade,
And you, but one, can every shadow lend.   *4*
Describe Adonis, and the counterfeit
Is poorly imitated after you;
On Helen's cheek all art of beauty set,
And you in Grecian tires are painted new.   *8*
Speak of the spring and foison of the year;
The one doth shadow of your beauty show,
The other as your bounty doth appear,
And you in every blessèd shape we know.   *12*
   In all external grace you have some part,
    But you like none, none you, for constant heart.

O, how much more doth beauty beauteous seem,
By that sweet ornament which truth doth give!
The rose looks fair, but fairer we it deem
For that sweet odor which doth in it live.   *4*
The canker blooms have full as deep a dye,
As the perfumèd tincture of the roses,
Hang on such thorns, and play as wantonly,
When summer's breath their maskèd buds discloses; *8*
But, for their virtue only is their show,
They live unwooed and unrespected fade,
Die to themselves. Sweet roses do not so;
Of their sweet deaths are sweetest odors made.   *12*
   And so of you, beauteous and lovely youth,
    When that shall vade, by verse distills your truth.

Being your slave, what should I do but tend
Upon the hours and times of your desire?
I have no precious time at all to spend,
Nor services to do till you require.   *4*
Nor dare I chide the world-without-end hour
Whilst I, my sovereign, watch the clock for you,
Nor think the bitterness of absence sour
When you have bid your servant once adieu.   *8*
Nor dare I question with my jealous thought
Where you may be, or your affairs suppose,
But, like a sad slave, stay and think of naught
Save where you are how happy you make those.   *12*
    So true a fool is love that in your will,
    Though you do anything, he thinks no ill.

Like as the waves make towards the pebbled shore,
So do our minutes hasten to their end;
Each changing place with that which goes before,
In sequent toil all forwards do contend.   4
Nativity, once in the main of light,
Crawls to maturity, wherewith being crowned,
Crooked eclipses 'gainst his glory fight,
And Time that gave doth now his gift confound.   8
Time doth transfix the flourish set on youth,
And delves the parallels in beauty's brow,
Feeds on the rarities of nature's truth,
And nothing stands but for his scythe to mow: 12
    And yet to times in hope my verse shall stand,
    Praising thy worth, despite his cruel hand.

Is it thy will thy image should keep open
My heavy eyelids to the weary night?
Dost thou desire my slumbers should be broken
While shadows like to thee do mock my sight?   *4*
Is it thy spirit that thou send'st from thee
So far from home into my deeds to pry,
To find out shames and idle hours in me,
The scope and tenure of thy jealousy?   *8*
O no, thy love, though much, is not so great.
It is my love that keeps mine eye awake,
Mine own true love that doth my rest defeat,
To play the watchman ever for thy sake.   *12*
   For thee watch I, whilst thou dost wake elsewhere,
   From me far off, with others all too near.

Tired with all these, for restful death I cry,
As, to behold desert a beggar born,
And needy nothing trimmed in jollity,
And purest faith unhappily forsworn, *4*
And gilded honor shamefully misplaced,
And maiden virtue rudely strumpeted,
And right perfection wrongfully disgraced,
And strength by limping sway disabled, *8*
And art made tongue-tied by authority,
And folly (doctorlike) controlling skill,
And simple truth miscalled simplicity,
And captive good attending captain ill. *12*
    Tired with all these, from these would I be gone,
    Save that to die, I leave my love alone.

No longer mourn for me when I am dead
Than you shall hear the surly sullen bell
Give warning to the world that I am fled
From this vile world with vilest worms to dwell.   *4*
Nay, if you read this line, remember not
The hand that writ it, for I love you so
That I in your sweet thoughts would be forgot,
If thinking on me then should make you woe.   *8*
O, if, I say, you look upon this verse,
When I, perhaps, compounded am with clay,
Do not so much as my poor name rehearse,
But let your love even with my life decay,   *12*
    Lest the wise world should look into your moan,
    And mock you with me after I am gone.

74

But be contented. When that fell arrest
Without all bail shall carry me away,
My life hath in this line some interest
Which for memorial still with thee shall stay.   *4*
When thou reviewest this, thou dost review
The very part was consecrate to thee.
The earth can have but earth, which is his due;
My spirit is thine, the better part of me.   *8*
So then thou hast but lost the dregs of life,
The prey of worms, my body being dead;
The coward conquest of a wretch's knife,
Too base of thee to be remembered.   *12*
  The worth of that is that which it contains,
  And that is this, and this with thee remains.

Thy glass will show thee how thy beauties wear,
Thy dial how thy precious minutes waste;
The vacant leaves thy mind's imprint will bear,
And of this book this learning mayst thou taste.   *4*
The wrinkles which thy glass will truly show,
Of mouthèd graves, will give thee memory;
Thou by thy dial's shady stealth mayst know
Time's thievish progress to eternity.   *8*
Look what thy memory cannot contain,
Commit to these waste blanks, and thou shalt find
Those children nursed, delivered from thy brain,
To take a new acquaintance of thy mind.   *12*
   These offices, so oft as thou wilt look,
    Shall profit thee, and much enrich thy book.

Whilst I alone did call upon thy aid,
My verse alone had all thy gentle grace;
But now my gracious numbers are decayed,
And my sick Muse doth give another place.   *4*
I grant, sweet love, thy lovely argument
Deserves the travail of a worthier pen,
Yet what of thee thy poet doth invent
He robs thee of, and pays it thee again.   *8*
He lends thee virtue, and he stole that word
From thy behavior; beauty doth he give,
And found it in thy cheek; he can afford
No praise to thee but what in thee doth live.   *12*
  Then thank him not for that which he doth say,
  Since what he owes thee thou thyself dost pay.

O, how I faint when I of you do write,
Knowing a better spirit doth use your name,
And in the praise thereof spends all his might,
To make me tongue-tied speaking of your fame. *4*
But since your worth, wide as the ocean is,
The humble as the proudest sail doth bear,
My saucy bark, inferior far to his,
On your broad main doth willfully appear. *8*
Your shallowest help will hold me up afloat
Whilst he upon your soundless deep doth ride;
Or, being wracked, I am a worthless boat,
He of tall building, and of goodly pride. *12*

    Then if he thrive, and I be cast away,
      The worst was this: my love was my decay.

Was it the proud full sail of his great verse,
Bound for the prize of all too precious you,
That did my ripe thoughts in my brain inhearse,
Making their tomb the womb wherein they grew?   *4*
Was it his spirit, by spirits taught to write
Above a mortal pitch, that struck me dead?
No, neither he, nor his compeers by night
Giving him aid, my verse astonishèd.   *8*
He, nor that affable familiar ghost
Which nightly gulls him with intelligence,
As victors, of my silence cannot boast;
I was not sick of any fear from thence.   *12*
    But when your countenance filled up his line,
    Then lacked I matter, that enfeebled mine.

Farewell, thou are too dear for my possessing,
And like enough thou know'st thy estimate.
The charter of thy worth gives thee releasing;
My bonds in thee are all determinate.   *4*
For how do I hold thee but by thy granting,
And for that riches where is my deserving?
The cause of this fair gift in me is wanting,
And so my patent back again is swerving.   *8*
Thyself thou gav'st, thy own worth then not knowing,
Or me, to whom thou gav'st it, else mistaking;
So thy great gift, upon misprision growing,
Comes home again, on better judgment making.   *12*
   Thus have I had thee as a dream doth flatter,
   In sleep a king, but waking no such matter.

Say that thou didst forsake me for some fault,
And I will comment upon that offense.
Speak of my lameness, and I straight will halt,
Against thy reasons making no defense.   *4*
Thou canst not, love, disgrace me half so ill,
To set a form upon desirèd change,
As I'll myself disgrace, knowing thy will.
I will acquaintance strangle and look strange;   *8*
Be absent from thy walks, and in my tongue
Thy sweet belovèd name no more shall dwell,
Lest I, too much profane, should do it wrong
And haply of our old acquaintance tell.   *12*
    For thee, against myself I'll vow debate,
    For I must ne'er love him whom thou dost hate.

They that have pow'r to hurt and will do none,
That do not do the thing they most do show,
Who, moving others, are themselves as stone,
Unmovèd, cold, and to temptation slow;   *4*
They rightly do inherit heaven's graces
And husband nature's riches from expense;
They are the lords and owners of their faces,
Others but stewards of their excellence.   *8*
The summer's flow'r is to the summer sweet,
Though to itself it only live and die;
But if that flow'r with base infection meet,
The basest weed outbraves his dignity: *12*
    For sweetest things turn sourest by their deeds;
    Lilies that fester smell far worse than weeds.

Some say thy fault is youth, some wantonness,
Some say thy grace is youth and gentle sport;
Both grace and faults are loved of more and less;
Thou mak'st faults graces that to thee resort.　　*4*
As on the finger of a thronèd queen
The basest jewel will be well esteemed,
So are those errors that in thee are seen
To truths translated and for true things deemed.　　*8*
How many lambs might the stern wolf betray,
If like a lamb he could his looks translate;
How many gazers might'st thou lead away,
If thou wouldst use the strength of all thy state!　　*12*
　But do not so; I love thee in such sort
　As, thou being mine, mine is thy good report.

How like a winter hath my absence been
From thee, the pleasure of the fleeting year!
What freezings have I felt, what dark days seen,
What old December's bareness everywhere!   *4*
And yet this time removed was summer's time,
The teeming autumn, big with rich increase,
Bearing the wanton burden of the prime,
Like widowed wombs after their lords' decease.   *8*
Yet this abundant issue seemed to me
But hope of orphans and unfathered fruit;
For summer and his pleasures wait on thee,
And, thou away, the very birds are mute;   *12*
   Or, if they sing, 'tis with so dull a cheer,
    That leaves look pale, dreading the winter's near.

The forward violet thus did I chide:
Sweet thief, whence didst thou steal thy sweet that smells
If not from my love's breath? The purple pride
Which on thy soft cheek for complexion dwells   *4*
In my love's veins thou hast too grossly dyed.
The lily I condemnèd for thy hand,
And buds of marjoram had stol'n thy hair;
The roses fearfully on thorns did stand,   *8*
One blushing shame, another white despair;
A third, nor red nor white, had stol'n of both,
And to his robb'ry had annexed thy breath;
But for his theft, in pride of all his growth   *12*
A vengeful canker eat him up to death.
   More flowers I noted, yet I none could see,
   But sweet or color it had stol'n from thee.

To me, fair friend, you never can be old,
For as you were when first your eye I eyed,
Such seems your beauty still. Three winters cold
Have from the forests shook three summers' pride,   *4*
Three beauteous springs to yellow autumn turned
In process of the seasons have I seen,
Three April perfumes in three hot Junes burned,
Since first I saw you fresh, which yet are green.   *8*
Ah, yet doth beauty, like a dial hand,
Steal from his figure, and no pace perceived;
So your sweet hue, which methinks still doth stand,
Hath motion, and mine eye may be deceived;   *12*
  For fear of which, hear this, thou age unbred:
  Ere you were born was beauty's summer dead.

Let not my love be called idolatry,
Nor my belovèd as an idol show,
Since all alike my songs and praises be
To one, of one, still such, and ever so.   *4*
Kind is my love today, tomorrow kind,
Still constant in a wondrous excellence;
Therefore my verse, to constancy confined,
One thing expressing, leaves out difference.   *8*
Fair, kind, and true is all my argument,
Fair, kind, and true, varying to other words;
And in this change is my invention spent,
Three themes in one, which wondrous scope affords.   *12*
  Fair, kind, and true have often lived alone,
  Which three till now never kept seat in one.

When in the chronicle of wasted time
I see descriptions of the fairest wights,
And beauty making beautiful old rhyme
In praise of ladies dead and lovely knights;   *4*
Then, in the blazon of sweet beauty's best,
Of hand, of foot, of lip, of eye, of brow,
I see their antique pen would have expressed
Even such a beauty as you master now.   *8*
So all their praises are but prophecies
Of this our time, all you prefiguring,
And, for they looked but with divining eyes,
They had not still enough your worth to sing: *12*
    For we, which now behold these present days,
    Have eyes to wonder, but lack tongues to praise.

Not mine own fears nor the prophetic soul
Of the wide world dreaming on things to come
Can yet the lease of my true love control,
Supposed as forfeit to a confined doom.   *4*
The mortal moon hath her eclipse endured,
And the sad augurs mock their own presage,
Incertainties now crown themselves assured,
And peace proclaims olives of endless age.   *8*
Now with the drops of this most balmy time
My love looks fresh, and Death to me subscribes,
Since, spite of him, I'll live in this poor rhyme,
While he insults o'er dull and speechless tribes: *12*
   And thou in this shalt find thy monument,
    When tyrants' crests and tombs of brass are spent.

Alas, 'tis true I have gone here and there
And made myself a motley to the view,
Gored mine own thoughts, sold cheap what is most dear,
Made old offenses of affections new. 4
Most true it is that I have looked on truth
Askance and strangely; but, by all above,
These blenches gave my heart another youth,
And worse essays proved thee my best of love. 8
Now all is done, have what shall have no end.
Mine appetite I never more will grind
On newer proof, to try an older friend,
A god in love, to whom I am confined. 12
    Then give me welcome, next my heaven the best,
    Even to thy pure and most loving breast.

Those lines that I before have writ do lie,
Even those that said I could not love you dearer.
Yet then my judgment knew no reason why
My most full flame should afterwards burn clearer. *4*
But reckoning Time, whose millioned accidents
Creep in 'twixt vows and change decrees of kings,
Tan sacred beauty, blunt the sharp'st intents,
Divert strong minds to th' course of alt'ring things. *8*
Alas, why, fearing of Time's tyranny,
Might I not then say, "Now I love you best,"
When I was certain o'er incertainty,
Crowning the present, doubting of the rest? *12*
    Love is a babe; then might I not say so,
      To give full growth to that which still doth grow.

Let me not to the marriage of true minds
Admit impediments; love is not love
Which alters when it alteration finds,
Or bends with the remover to remove.　　　　4
O, no, it is an ever-fixèd mark
That looks on tempests and is never shaken;
It is the star to every wand'ring bark,
Whose worth's unknown, although his height be taken.　　8
Love's not Time's fool, though rosy lips and cheeks
Within his bending sickle's compass come;
Love alters not with his brief hours and weeks,
But bears it out even to the edge of doom.　　　　12
　　If this be error and upon me proved,
　　I never writ, nor no man ever loved.

What potions have I drunk of Siren tears
Distilled from limbecks foul as hell within,
Applying fears to hopes and hopes to fears,
Still losing when I saw myself to win!   *4*
What wretched errors hath my heart committed,
Whilst it hath thought itself so blessèd never!
How have mine eyes out of their spheres been fitted
In the distraction of this madding fever!   *8*
O, benefit of ill: now I find true
That better is by evil still made better;
And ruined love, when it is built anew,
Grows fairer than at first, more strong, far greater.   *12*
   So I return rebuked to my content,
    And gain by ills thrice more than I have spent.

Thy gift, thy tables, are within my brain
Full charactered with lasting memory,
Which shall above that idle rank remain
Beyond all date, even to eternity;   *4*
Or, at the least, so long as brain and heart
Have faculty by nature to subsist,
Till each to rased oblivion yield his part
Of thee, thy record never can be missed.   *8*
That poor retention could not so much hold,
Nor need I tallies thy dear love to score.
Therefore to give them from me was I bold,
To trust those tables that receive thee more.   *12*
   To keep an adjunct to remember thee
   Were to import forgetfulness in me.

No, Time, thou shalt not boast that I do change.
Thy pyramids built up with newer might
To me are nothing novel, nothing strange;
They are but dressings of a former sight.   *4*
Our dates are brief, and therefore we admire
What thou dost foist upon us that is old,
And rather make them born to our desire
Than think that we before have heard them told.   *8*
Thy registers and thee I both defy,
Not wond'ring at the present, nor the past;
For thy records and what we see doth lie,
Made more or less by thy continual haste.   *12*
   This I do vow, and this shall ever be:
   I will be true despite thy scythe and thee.

If my dear love were but the child of state,
It might for Fortune's bastard be unfathered,
As subject to Time's love, or to Time's hate,
Weeds among weeds, or flowers with flowers gathered.   *4*
No, it was builded far from accident;
It suffers not in smiling pomp, nor falls
Under the blow of thrallèd discontent,
Whereto th' inviting time our fashion calls.   *8*
It fears not Policy, that heretic,
Which works on leases of short-numb'red hours,
But all alone stands hugely politic,
That it nor grows with heat, nor drowns with showers.   *12*
    To this I witness call the fools of Time,
     Which die for goodness, who have lived for crime.

Were't aught to me I bore the canopy,
With my extern the outward honoring,
Or laid great bases for eternity,
Which proves more short than waste or ruining? *4*
Have I not seen dwellers on form and favor
Lose all and more by paying too much rent,
For compound sweet forgoing simple savor,
Pitiful thrivers, in their gazing spent? *8*
No, let me be obsequious in thy heart,
And take thou my oblation, poor but free,
Which is not mixed with seconds, knows no art,
But mutual render, only me for thee. *12*
   Hence, thou suborned informer! A true soul
    When most impeached stands least in thy control.

O thou, my lovely boy, who in thy power
Dost hold Time's fickle glass, his sickle hour,
Who hast by waning grown, and therein show'st
Thy lovers withering, as thy sweet self grow'st;   *4*
If Nature, sovereign mistress over wrack,
As thou goest onwards, still will pluck thee back,
She keeps thee to this purpose, that her skill
May Time disgrace and wretched minutes kill.   *8*
Yet fear her, O thou minion of her pleasure;
She may detain, but not still keep her treasure.
   Her audit, though delayed, answered must be,
   And her quietus is to render thee.   *12*

In the old age black was not counted fair,
Or, if it were, it bore not beauty's name.
But now is black beauty's successive heir,
And beauty slandered with a bastard shame;   4
For since each hand hath put on nature's power,
Fairing the foul with art's false borrowed face,
Sweet beauty hath no name, no holy bower,
But is profaned, if not lives in disgrace.   8
Therefore my mistress' eyes are raven black,
Her eyes so suited, and they mourners seem,
At such who, not born fair, no beauty lack,
Sland'ring creation with a false esteem: 12
    Yet so they mourn, becoming of their woe,
    That every tongue says beauty should look so.

My mistress' eyes are nothing like the sun;
Coral is far more red than her lips' red;
If snow be white, why then her breasts are dun;
If hairs be wires, black wires grow on her head.   *4*
I have seen roses damasked, red and white,
But no such roses see I in her cheeks,
And in some perfumes is there more delight
Than in the breath that from my mistress reeks.   *8*
I love to hear her speak, yet well I know
That music hath a far more pleasing sound.
I grant I never saw a goddess go;
My mistress when she walks treads on the ground.   *12*
    And yet, by heaven, I think my love as rare
    As any she belied with false compare.

Thine eyes I love, and they, as pitying me,
Knowing thy heart torment me with disdain,
Have put on black and loving mourners be,
Looking with pretty ruth upon my pain.   *4*
And truly not the morning sun of heaven
Better becomes the gray cheeks of the east,
Nor that full star that ushers in the even
Doth half that glory to the sober west   *8*
As those two mourning eyes become thy face.
O, let it then as well beseem thy heart
To mourn for me, since mourning doth thee grace,
And suit thy pity like in every part.   *12*
    Then will I swear beauty herself is black,
      And all they foul that thy complexion lack.

Beshrew that heart that makes my heart to groan
For that deep wound it gives my friend and me.
Is't not enough to torture me alone,
But slave to slavery my sweet'st friend must be? 4
Me from myself thy cruel eye hath taken,
And my next self thou harder hast engrossed.
Of him, myself, and thee, I am forsaken;
A torment thrice threefold thus to be crossed. 8
Prison my heart in thy steel bosom's ward,
But then my friend's heart let my poor heart bail;
Whoe'er keeps me, let my heart be his guard;
Thou canst not then use rigor in my jail. 12
    And yet thou wilt, for I, being pent in thee,
      Perforce am thine, and all that is in me.

So, now I have confessed that he is thine
And I myself am mortgaged to thy will,
Myself I'll forfeit, so that other mine
Thou wilt restore to be my comfort still.   *4*
But thou wilt not, nor he will not be free,
For thou art covetous, and he is kind;
He learned but surety-like to write for me
Under that bond that him as fast doth bind.   *8*
The statute of thy beauty thou wilt take,
Thou usurer that put'st forth all to use,
And sue a friend came debtor for my sake;
So him I lose through my unkind abuse.   *12*
  Him have I lost, thou hast both him and me;
  He pays the whole, and yet am I not free.

Whoever hath her wish, thou hast thy *Will*,
And *Will* to boot, and *Will* in overplus;
More than enough am I that vex thee still,
To thy sweet will making addition thus.   *4*
Wilt thou, whose will is large and spacious
Not once vouchsafe to hide my will in thine?
Shall will in others seem right gracious,
And in my will no fair acceptance shine?   *8*
The sea, all water, yet receives rain still
And in abundance addeth to his store;
So thou being rich in *Will* add to thy *Will*
One will of mine, to make thy large *Will* more.   *12*
   Let no unkind, no fair beseechers kill;
   Think all but one, and me in that one *Will*.

137

Thou blind fool, Love, what dost thou to mine eyes
That they behold and see not what they see?
They know what beauty is, see where it lies,
Yet what the best is take the worst to be.   4
If eyes, corrupt by overpartial looks,
Be anchored in the bay where all men ride,
Why of eyes' falsehood has thou forgèd hooks,
Whereto the judgment of my heart is tied?   8
Why should my heart think that a several plot,
Which my heart knows the wide world's common place?
Or mine eyes seeing this, say this is not,
To put fair truth upon so foul a face?   12
  In things right true my heart and eyes have erred,
  And to this false plague are they now transferred.

When my love swears that she is made of truth,
I do believe her though I know she lies,
That she might think me some untutored youth,
Unlearnèd in the world's false subtleties.   *4*
Thus vainly thinking that she thinks me young,
Although she knows my days are past the best,
Simply I credit her false-speaking tongue;
On both sides thus is simple truth suppressed.   *8*
But wherefore says she not she is unjust?
And wherefore say not I that I am old?
O, love's best habit is in seeming trust,
And age in love loves not to have years told.   *12*
    Therefore I lie with her, and she with me,
    And in our faults by lies we flattered be.

In faith I do not love thee with mine eyes,
For they in thee a thousand errors note;
But 'tis my heart that loves what they despise,
Who in despite of view is pleased to dote.   *4*
Nor are mine ears with thy tongue's tune delighted,
Nor tender feeling to base touches prone,
Nor taste, nor smell, desire to be invited
To any sensual feast with thee alone.   *8*
But my five wits nor my five senses can
Dissuade one foolish heart from serving thee,
Who leaves unswayed the likeness of a man,
Thy proud heart's slave and vassal wretch to be.   *12*
   Only my plague thus far I count my gain,
   That she that makes me sin awards me pain.

Lo, as a careful housewife runs to catch
One of her feathered creatures broke away,
Sets down her babe, and makes all swift dispatch
In pursuit of the thing she would have stay;   *4*
Whilst her neglected child holds her in chase,
Cries to catch her whose busy care is bent
To follow that which flies before her face,
Not prizing her poor infant's discontent: *8*
So run'st thou after that which flies from thee,
Whilst I, thy babe, chase thee afar behind;
But if thou catch thy hope, turn back to me
And play the mother's part, kiss me, be kind.   *12*

    So will I pray that thou mayst have thy *Will*,
    If thou turn back and my loud crying still.

Two loves I have, of comfort and despair,
Which like two spirits do suggest me still;
The better angel is a man right fair,
The worser spirit a woman colored ill.   *4*
To win me soon to hell, my female evil
Tempteth my better angel from my side,
And would corrupt my saint to be a devil,
Wooing his purity with her foul pride.   *8*
And whether that my angel be turned fiend
Suspect I may, yet not directly tell;
But being both from me, both to each friend,
I guess one angel in another's hell.   *12*
   Yet this shall I ne'er know, but live in doubt,
   Till my bad angel fire my good one out.

Those lips that Love's own hand did make
Breathed forth the sound that said, "I hate"
To me that languished for her sake.
But when she saw my woeful state,   *4*
Straight in her heart did mercy come,
Chiding that tongue that ever sweet
Was used in giving gentle doom,
And taught it thus anew to greet: *8*
"I hate," she altered with an end
That followed it as gentle day
Doth follow night, who, like a fiend,
From heaven to hell is flown away.   *12*
   "I hate" from hate away she threw,
    And saved my life, saying, "not you."

My love is as a fever, longing still
For that which longer nurseth the disease,
Feeding on that which doth preserve the ill,
Th' uncertain sickly appetite to please.   *4*
My reason, the physician to my love,
Angry that his prescriptions are not kept,
Hath left me, and I desperate now approve
Desire is death, which physic did except.   *8*
Past cure I am, now reason is past care,
And frantic-mad with evermore unrest;
My thoughts and my discourse as madmen's are,
At random from the truth vainly expressed: *12*
    For I have sworn thee fair, and thought thee bright,
    Who art as black as hell, as dark as night.

O, from what pow'r hast thou this pow'rful might
With insufficiency my heart to sway?
To make me give the lie to my true sight
And swear that brightness doth not grace the day?   *4*
Whence hast thou this becoming of things ill
That in the very refuse of thy deeds
There is such strength and warrantize of skill
That in my mind thy worst all best exceeds?   *8*
Who taught thee how to make me love thee more,
The more I hear and see just cause of hate?
O, though I love what others do abhor,
With others thou shouldst not abhor my state: *12*
    If thy unworthiness raised love in me,
    More worthy I to be beloved of thee.

Love is too young to know what conscience is,
Yet who knows not conscience is born of love?
Then, gentle cheater, urge not my amiss,
Lest guilty of my faults thy sweet self prove.⠀⠀⠀⠀⠀4
For, thou betraying me, I do betray
My nobler part to my gross body's treason;
My soul doth tell my body that he may
Triumph in love; flesh stays no farther reason,⠀⠀8
But, rising at thy name, doth point out thee,
As his triumphant prize. Proud of this pride,
He is contented thy poor drudge to be,
To stand in thy affairs, fall by thy side.⠀⠀⠀⠀12
⠀⠀No want of conscience hold it that I call
⠀⠀Her "love" for whose dear love I rise and fall.

In loving thee thou know'st I am forsworn,
But thou art twice forsworn, to me love swearing;
In act thy bed-vow broke, and new faith torn
In vowing new hate after new love bearing.   *4*
But why of two oaths' breach do I accuse thee,
When I break twenty? I am perjured most,
For all my vows are oaths but to misuse thee,
And all my honest faith in thee is lost;   *8*
For I have sworn deep oaths of thy deep kindness,
Oaths of thy love, thy truth, thy constancy;
And, to enlighten thee, gave eyes to blindness,
Or made them swear against the thing they see;   *12*
    For I have sworn thee fair; more perjured eye,
    To swear against the truth so foul a lie.